A TRUCK NAMED TO

BY M. JANE HAWKINS

ILLUSTRATED BY DAVID BARROW

ISBN#978-0-9972351-8-0 (hard cover)

ISBN#978-0-9989302-0-6 (soft cover)

Book design by Marla F. Jones

Fonts used: VAG Rundschrift D, **TOONISH**, AR Destine, and AR Christy

Library of Congress Control Number: 2017930000

To Michael, the inspiration for Tony's story; and to Frank, the first person to introduce me as a writer.

Many thanks to the Society of Children's Book Writers and Illustrators for their resources for new writers. Thank you to SCBWI-OK, especially my Tulsa group, for welcoming me into the fold, encouraging me along my journey, and offering honest critiques of this story.

I want to thank the very smart women in my study group for giving me confidence and honest opinions. They nagged - oops, encouraged - me to press on and submit, submit, submit. They cheered for me along the publishing journey with the promise of champagne and apple pie at the finish line.

Finally, I want to thank my editor, Marla Jones, for seeing something in my story worth bringing to you.

M. Jane Hawkins

For my son, Jonathan. Watching you grow up and become so responsible has been one of my greatest pleasures.

David Barrow

Tony looked out the big window and watched the world go by. Every day, people opened and closed his doors and looked under his hood. Someone even dropped an ice cream cone on his tailgate.

A purple truck drove by. She had huge tires, a shiny bumper with a winch, and yellow flashing lights. Tony nudged the sports car next to him. "Mikey, that truck can go on bumpy roads, through tall grass, up hills and down valleys. She can even help cars get out of the mud!" He sighed. "I've never even been outside."

"Quit daydreaming," said Mikey. "Someone's coming over."

The man raised Tony's hood and kicked his tires.

Then he jiggled the keys and started Tony's engine.

But the man only drove down the block. Then he brought Tony back.

Tony frowned.

"Don't worry your water pump, buddy," said Mikey. "Someone will pick you."

A cowboy sauntered over. He dropped Tony's tailgate and honked Tony's horn. Then they went for a drive.

But the cowboy brought him back, too.

"Don't bust your battery," said Mikey. "Your turn will come."

The next day a woman came into the showroom and walked straight to Tony.

"Oh, I love red!" She drove Tony around the block.

Back at the showroom, the woman threw up her hands and said, "Oh...I just can't decide!" She walked out.

Tony's fenders drooped.

Tony stopped looking out the big window.

He quit talking to Mikey.

He even gave up dreaming about bumpy roads and tall grass.

On Saturday, Mikey jabbed Tony. "Quit moping. I've got a good feeling about them."

The family walked over, opened and closed Tony's doors, and looked under his hood.

The boy dropped his ice cream cone on Tony's tailgate. But he cleaned it right up.

Then the whole family piled inside and took him for a drive.

Tony whispered, "Pick me, pick me, pick me."

FREE ICE CREAM

And they did.

Tony loved driving the man to work,

and going on camping trips,

and starring in parades.

When he was with the family, Tony sparkled and giggled.

After a few years,
Tony's brakes didn't work so well,
    his paint had chipped and faded,
        and he coughed all the time.
One day he heard a familiar voice. "Sputtering spark plugs, is that you, Tony? You sound awful." It was Mikey!

"I know," muttered Tony. "They're going to buy a new truck."

That night, Tony whispered, "Please, don't forget me."

And he dreamed about the purple truck, bumpy roads and tall grass.

Once in a while, the boy brushed off Tony's cobwebs and polished his chrome.

Tony would glow.

But when the boy left, Tony's tires went flat.

Then one day, the boy looked under Tony's hood and started his engine.

COUGH...S-S-SPUTTER. Tony backfired.

POW!

"Please don't take me to the junk yard. Please, please, please."

A mechanic fixed Tony's brakes and tuned his engine.
Then Tony was covered with fresh paint.

Before long, Tony **bopped and bounced** over bumpy roads,

jiggled and jostled through tall grass, and

zigged and *zagged*

up hills and **down** valleys.

He even helped cars get out of the mud.

"Poppin' pistons!" yelled Tony. "What a dandy, dynamite day!"

And every time they passed the purple truck, Tony beeped his horn.
The boy didn't mind. He just winked and smiled.

So did Tony.

AUTHOR
M. Jane Hawkins

ILLUSTRATOR
David Barrow

M. Jane Hawkins has been a junior high English teacher, a stay-at-home mom, and an employee at a regional magazine where she sold advertisements, wrote and edited articles, and eventually, became editor. She has been a reading mentor for children and helped students start a newspaper club. **A Truck Named Tony** is her first picture book.

David Barrow spent his happiest hours in the school library. It was there he read books about famous people and learned how to draw. After working as a graphic designer, camera man, video editor, and illustrator, David embarked on his lifelong dream of illustrating children's books.

This is Barrows second picture book with Doodle and Peck Publishing.